Meet Moana

This is Moana. She lives on a beautiful island in the middle of the ocean. She is a strong and determined girl who is destined to be the island's leader someday. Let's find out more about Moana and her world!

Where does Moana live?

The island of Motunui.
Motunui is covered with plants, trees, and waterfalls. A coral reef surrounds the island and creates a calm lagoon for fishing. The island gives the people of Motunui everything they need.

What is special about Moana's family?

Her father is the island chief. Moana is going to take over as the island chief one day.

Who lives on Motunui?

Moana, her parents, Gramma Tala, and many other villagers.

The villagers of Motunui share the island with cute creatures, such as pigs and chickens.

Who follows Moana around the island?

Pua. This spotted piglet trots after Moana almost everywhere she goes. Moana loves her loyal friend.

Where is the village?

Near the lagoon and fields where the villagers grow food. The villagers' homes are surrounded by coconut palms and clear freshwater streams. Motunui is paradise. Who would ever want to leave?

What type of tree is important to the village?

Coconut palms. These tropical trees grow all over Motunui. The villagers use parts of the trees to weave fishing nets and build fires. They eat the coconuts and drink the coconut water.

How many different plants grow on Motunui?

About 40 types of plants.

Moana loves the colorful flowers that grow on Motunui. Sometimes she wears a pink plumeria in her hair!

What do the villagers catch in the reef?

Fish. There have always been plenty of fish for the villagers to catch in the reef. But lately, there haven't been as many fish there. What could be happening?

How do the villagers cook?

With open fires. The people of Motunui cook their fish over big open fires. Moana loves to share food and spend time with the other villagers.

What is Moana's favorite snack?

Fresh fruit. Moana enjoys juicy pineapples and ripe bananas. The island has plenty of delicious foods for the villagers to eat.

What types of houses do the villagers live in?

Fales. Each fale is home to a group of families from the village. Moana and her family live in a fale that is similar to this one.

Who lives in Moana's fale?

Moana's mother, father, and Gramma Tala.

Moana's house is the biggest in the village because her father is the chief. There is plenty of room for friends like Pua, too.

What story does Gramma Tala tell Moana?

The legend of Te Fiti's heart.

Te Fiti is the mother island that creates life. Many years ago, a demigod named Maui stole Te Fiti's heart. A darkness then spread and drained the life from all the islands. Moana has heard this tale many times, but could it be true?

Where does Moana like to spend time?

Upstairs. Moana can see the ocean from here! Away from everyone else, she can dream about anything her heart desires.

What is Moana's dream?

To explore the ocean.

Moana feels that the ocean is calling her.
She wants to sail beyond the reef, but her
father thinks it is too dangerous.

What first led Moana to the ocean?

A baby sea turtle.
When Moana was a toddler, she showed her kindness by helping a baby sea turtle get to the safety of the water. That day, the ocean gave Moana something very special—Te Fiti's heart!

23

What is happening to the crops on Motunui?

They are starting to die. No one knows why, but the coconuts are turning black! Little by little, fish, fruit, and other crops are disappearing. Moana is determined to help.

How does Moana think she can help the village?

By sailing beyond the reef. Moana thinks that she can find fish in deeper water. Her father tells her that no one on the island is allowed to sail beyond the reef. It is too risky.

25

Does Moana listen to her father's warning?

No. She tries to sail out to sea.

Unluckily for Moana, an enormous
wave knocks her off her canoe.
Moana goes back to the beach
where Gramma Tala has
seen everything!

©2019
The LEGO Group

Where does Gramma Tala take Moana?

The cavern of the wayfinders.

Gramma Tala knows about Moana's wish to explore the ocean. She takes her to a secret cave to teach Moana about her ancestors.

What does Moana find inside?

Boats! Moana finds out that her ancestors were wayfinders. They sailed from Motunui across the ocean to look for new islands. Moana is excited to learn this!

What has Gramma Tala been hiding?

The heart of Te Fiti. Moana was only young when the heart washed up on the beach in front of her. Gramma Tala kept it hidden and safe for many years. Now she knows Moana is ready to look after the heart herself.

What does Moana find out about the heart of Te Fiti?

The legend is real! Without her heart, Te Fiti cannot create life. The darkness has spread to Motunui. If the heart is not restored, there will be no food, plants, or fish left!

What does the ocean want Moana to do?

◎ ◎ ◎

Restore the heart of Te Fiti. Moana was right! The ocean has been calling her. It chose her to take the heart back to the mother island and stop the darkness from spreading.

What family heirloom does Gramma Tala give to Moana?

A shell necklace. It once belonged to their voyager ancestors. Gramma Tala encourages Moana to go on her voyage to save Motunui. She promises to always be with her in spirit.

What does Moana keep inside the shell necklace?

The heart of Te Fiti. Moana knows that it is important to keep the heart of Te Fiti safe during her journey. The heart fits perfectly inside Gramma Tala's necklace.

©2019
The LEGO Group

Where must Moana sail?

To the island of Te Fiti.

Moana must sail on a canoe to restore the heart. But first, she must find the demigod who stole it and convince him to help her put Te Fiti's heart back in its rightful place.

What kind of boat does Moana sail on?

An outrigger canoe. Moana takes the canoe from the cavern. The boat is just the right size for Moana. It might be small but it is strong.

What does Moana take onboard with her?

Food. Moana's mother helps her pack plenty of food like fresh fruit and coconuts for her voyage across the sea. She stores it in a hidden compartment.

Who does Moana find on her boat?

Heihei. There is a surprise in Moana's storage area! A rooster named Heihei from the village got stuck inside Moana's boat and joins her on her voyage.

What does Heihei try to eat?

Rocks. This silly rooster likes to swallow stones! However, Moana knows that there is more to Heihei than meets the eye.

Who stole the heart of Te Fiti?

Maui. The demigod wanted to give the heart to humans so that they could create life themselves. He learns that only Te Fiti can use its power.

Where does Moana find Maui?

On a small island. After he stole the
heart, Maui got trapped on a tiny island for
1,000 years! He cannot leave the island
because he does not have a boat.

What does Maui try to steal from Moana?

Her canoe. Maui wants to sail away on Moana's boat to find his fishhook. The fishhook is precious to him. It has been lost since he took Te Fiti's heart.

What is special about Maui's fishhook?

It is magical! Maui can change into different creatures with a swish of his fishhook. Moana helps him get it back so that Maui will help her in return.

Who sails the sea looking for Te Fiti's heart?

Kakamora. These tiny pirates attack if they want something... and they want Te Fiti's heart for themselves! The Kakamora try to take the heart from Maui and Moana.

What kind of armor do the Kakamora wear?

Coconut hulls. The Kakamora are fierce warriors with tough armor, weapons, and scary battle paint. With determination and courage, Maui and Moana manage to fight them off and sail away safely.

Who stops Moana and Maui from reaching Te Fiti?

Te Kā. The demon of earth and fire wants Te Fiti's heart for herself. She does not want Moana and Maui to sail or fly around her.

What does Te Kā throw at Moana and Maui?

Lava. Te Kā launches balls of hot lava at the pair. The monster also cracks Maui's magical fishhook and creates a massive wave to sweep Maui and Moana far away from her.

Who appears by Moana's boat?

Gramma Tala's spirit. After Te Kā defeats Moana and Maui, poor Moana is downhearted. But Gramma Tala's spirit suddenly appears as a manta ray! Gramma Tala kept her promise to be with Moana wherever she goes.

What does Gramma Tala give Moana?

Courage. Moana's grandmother reminds her that she is brave enough to reach Te Fiti. Moana sets sail and fights Te Kā with some help from Maui, too.

Who does Moana give the heart to?

Te Kā! Moana realizes that Te Kā is really Te Fiti! The green mother island became an angry volcano after her heart was stolen. When Moana places the heart in Te Kā's chest, the fiery monster transforms into Te Fiti once more.

Who mends Maui's fishhook?

Te Fiti. Maui is sorry for taking Te Fiti's heart. Te Fiti knows that he did not mean any harm. The kind-hearted goddess forgives Maui and uses her magic to repair Maui's hook.

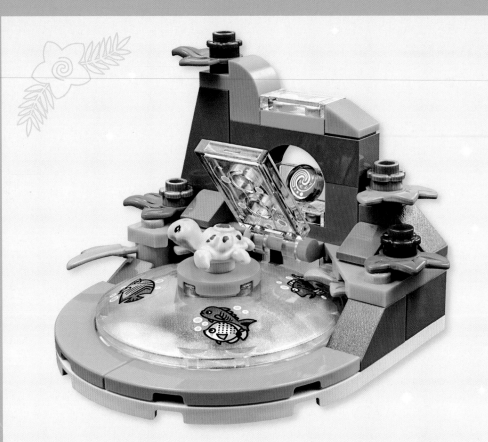

Has Moana succeeded?

Yes! The darkness has gone.

Now that Te Fiti's heart is back where it belongs, the mother island can create life again. Fish return to the reef, and plants, flowers, and food grow once more.

Where does Moana go next?

Home! Moana says goodbye to Te Fiti and Maui and sails back to Motunui. She cannot wait to see her family and the villagers again.

Is Moana's family angry with her?

No! Although she disobeyed her father he is still very proud of her. And most of all, Moana's parents are happy to see her home safely.

What happens on Motunui when Moana returns?

The people become wayfinders again. Moana has inspired the people to explore the ocean once more. There are so many adventures awaiting Moana, too!

Test your knowledge!

1. What is the name of Moana's island?

a) Motunui

b) Mitiaro

c) Manihiki

2. What important job does Moana's father have?

a) He is a police officer

b) He is the island chief

c) He is a top chef

3. Is Moana afraid of the ocean?

Yes—she never wants to leave the shore.

No—it is calling to her and she dreams of exploring it.

4. What does Moana discover about her ancestors?

a) That they were rich

b) That they were very tall

c) That they were wayfinders

5. Who hides the Heart of Te Fiti from Moana?

a) Gramma Tala

b) Kakamora

c) Maui

6. Where does Moana keep the Heart of Te Fiti?

a) In a diamond bracelet

b) In a shell necklace

c) Under her pillow

7. Is Maui able to use the Heart of Te Fiti's power?

Yes—its power is for everyone.

No—only Te Fiti can use its power.

8. Who launches hot lava at Moana and Maui?

a) Te Kā

b) Te Fiti

c) The Kakamora

Glossary

Convince
Make someone agree
to something

Crops
Plants that are grown for
food or another purpose

Demigod
Part human and part god

Destined
Set on a particular course

Fale
House with open sides
and a thatched roof

Heirloom
Something precious handed
down through the generations

Lagoon
Shallow body of salt water
by the ocean

Legend
Traditional story that is not
always based on real events

Restored
Put back again

Risky
Has the possibility of danger

Wayfinders
People who travel the
ocean guided by their
deep knowledge of the
sky and the water

Index

DK | Penguin Random House

Project Editor Lisa Stock
Senior Designer Lauren Adams
Senior Production Controller
Lloyd Robertson
Senior Production Editor
Jennifer Murray
Managing Editor Paula Regan
Managing Art Editor Jo Connor
Art Director Lisa Lanzarini
Publisher Julie Ferris
Publishing Director Mark Searle

Written by Julia March
Designed for DK by Elena Jarmoskaite

DK would like to thank Randi K. Sørensen,
Heidi K. Jensen, Paul Hansford, Martin
Leighton Lindhardt at the LEGO Group,
and Chelsea Alon at Disney. Thanks also to
Tali Stock for editorial assistance and
Lori Hand for proofreading.

First American Edition, 2021
Published in the United States by
DK Publishing
1450 Broadway, Suite 801, New York,
NY 10018

Page design copyright © 2021 Dorling
Kindersley Limited. DK, a Division of Penguin
Random House LLC
21 22 23 24 25 10 9 8 7 6 5 4 3 2 1
001–321867–May/2021

Manufactured by Dorling Kindersley
One Embassy Gardens, 8 Viaduct Gardens,
London SW11 7BW, under license from the
LEGO group.

A catalog record for this book
is available from the Library of Congress.
ISBN 978-0-7440-2855-3

DK books are available at special discounts
when purchased in bulk for sales promotions,
premiums, fund-raising, or educational use.
For details, contact: DK Publishing Special
Markets, 1450 Broadway, Suite 801,
New York, NY 10018
SpecialSales@dk.com

Printed and bound in China

For the curious
www.dk.com

MIX
Paper from
responsible sources
FSC™ C018179

This paper is made from
Forest Stewardship Council™
certified paper—one small
step in DK's commitment
to a sustainable future